HOW DO YOUR SENSES WORK?

Judy Tatchell

Illustrated by Maria Wheatley

Owwch!

Designed by Ruth Russell

Digital artwork by Fiona Johnson

What are senses?

Your body has lots of ways of finding out about the world around you. It uses things called senses. You have five senses.

YOUR FIVE SENSES
Seeing ✓
Hearing ✓
Touching ✓
Smelling ✓
Tasting ✓

...I think I'll stay away!!

Your eyes see things.

What's that??

Your ears hear things.

Ughh! Spit it out!!

Your tongue tastes things.

You're so soft...

Your skin feels things.

...mmm I'll eat some.

Your nose smells things.

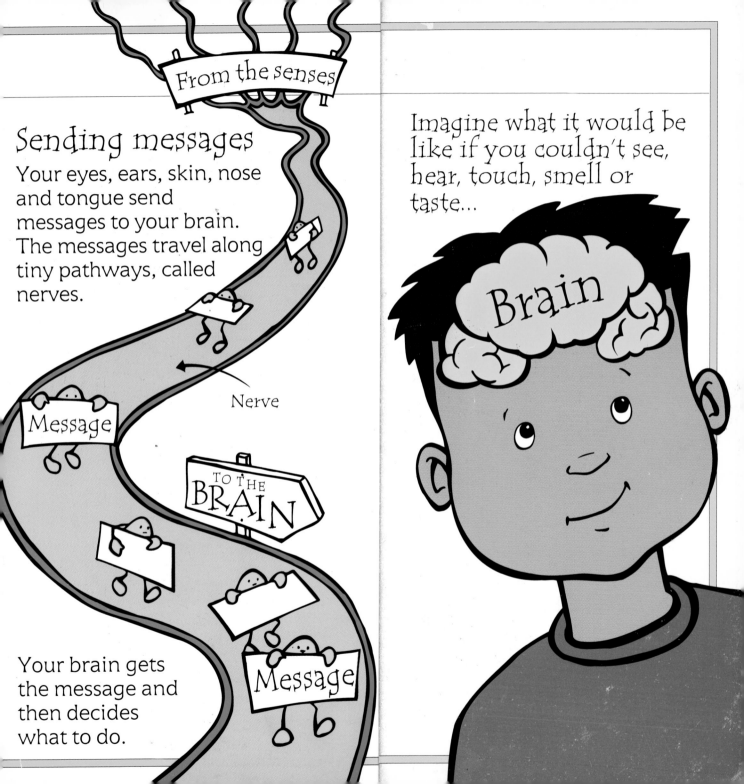

From the senses

Sending messages

Your eyes, ears, skin, nose and tongue send messages to your brain. The messages travel along tiny pathways, called nerves.

Nerve

Message

TO THE BRAIN

Message

Your brain gets the message and then decides what to do.

Imagine what it would be like if you couldn't see, hear, touch, smell or taste...

Brain

How do you see things?

You see with your eyes. They take moving pictures and send the pictures to your brain

How your eyes work

The black circle in the middle of each eye is a little hole. Light goes through the hole into your eye.

Light goes in here.

Inside, your eye makes a picture with the light.

Messages about the picture go down a nerve to your brain.

Eyes

Brain

Nerve

Message

That's MY bike!

Your brain understands the picture.

What are tears for?

Every time you blink, a few tears wash over each eye. They help to keep your eyes clean.

Blink!

When you cry, your eyes make lots of tears. No one knows why this happens.

Seeing in the dark

When it's dark you can't see much. Things look gray and murky...

But lift the flap and things look different!

How does hearing work?

You need ears to hear things. Just think what it would be like without ears.

Clean your room now!!

You wouldn't be able to listen to music.

Breep Breep

You wouldn't be able to hear people talking.

You wouldn't be able to hear the telephone.

Test your ears

Try this. Turn on the radio. Now shut your eyes and cover one ear. Turn around a few times. Can you tell where the radio is?

It is difficult to tell where sound is coming from with only one ear.

Your brain needs messages from both your ears.

Tweet

Chirrp

Crash

Miaow

Lift the flap to see inside your ear...

Touch

Your skin can feel things that it touches.

Your body can tell whether something is...

...hot ...or cold

...soft ...or hard

...tickly ...or scratchy.

Feeling things

Just inside your skin are lots of tiny touch receptors. They feel different things, and then send messages to your brain. They can feel...

...painful things

...tickly things

...hot things

...or cold things.

Oowwch!

Giggle

Whew it's hot!

Brrrr!

Good at feeling

Some parts of your body are better at feeling than others.

In this picture, the parts that can feel things very well are colored blue.

Parts that have lots of touch receptors in them can feel things very well.

How does touch work?

Lift the flap and see...

Buzzzz,

Buzzz

Smelling things

Your nose lets you know about all the good smells and bad smells around you.

How your nose works

You sniff in through your nose. The air zooms in. It's carrying a smell.

Sniff Whoosh

The air flows over a little patch high inside your nose. The patch has tiny hairs on it.

Hairs

Smell

Hairs

Message

The hairs send messages about the smell to your brain.

Brain

Message

Mmm... I like oranges

Blocked up nose

When you have a cold, lots and lots of gooey stuff is made in your nose. It is called mucus. It traps the germs in your nose.

The mucus covers the hairs that you use to smell things, too. It stops the smells from getting to the hairs.

I can't smell anything.

Nice and nasty smells

If you like the smell of food you will probably like the taste too. It makes you want to eat it.

Mmmm...

11

Tasting

Your tongue is your taster. It is covered in little bumps. You can just see them if you look closely. The bumps have taste buds on them. Taste buds sense different tastes.

Taste buds

There are four types of taste buds.

We taste sour things.

We taste bitter things.

We taste salty things.

We taste sweet things.

You taste different flavors with different parts of your tongue.

From tongue to brain

When food touches your taste buds, the taste buds send messages about its flavor to your brain.

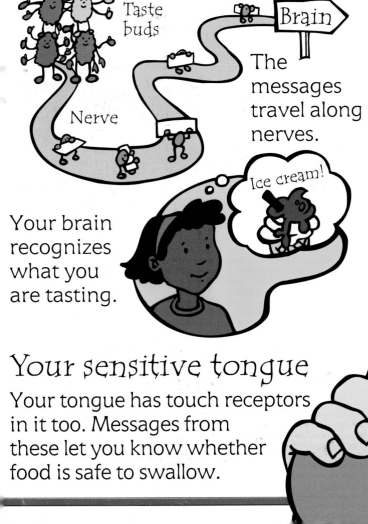

Taste buds

Nerve

Brain

The messages travel along nerves.

Your brain recognizes what you are tasting.

Ice cream!

Your sensitive tongue

Your tongue has touch receptors in it too. Messages from these let you know whether food is safe to swallow.

I'm hungry...

Clever senses

It's not just people who have senses. Animals have senses too. Some work better than yours.

Cats can see things much better than you can in the dark.

I spy a mouse!

What's the cat up to?

Eeeeek!

Dogs can smell things much better than you can. A dog can smell things that you can't.

sniff sniff

Ah - there's another dog nearby...

Ho - hum, nothing else around...

Sensitive skin

Some fish can sense through their skin if another fish is near. It tells them that their next meal might be close...

...or that they could be in danger from something else.

Senses all together

When you are awake, all your senses work at the same time. You can take in lots and lots of information at once, which can be useful...

Index

With thanks to Alastair Smith.
First published in 1997 by Usborne Publishing Ltd, 83-85 Saffron Hill, London EC1N 8RT, England.
First published in America March 1998. AE
Copyright © 1997 Usborne Publishing Ltd.